TRANS FORMERS

P R I M E

airachnid attacks!

BANTAM BOOKS

... :CHNID ATTACKS!
... 751146 1

... n by Bantam
... ren's Publishers UK
... Company

... 2

MIX
Paper from
responsible sources
FSC
www.fsc.org FSC® C016897

Set in 15/20pt Bembo Regular

Bantam Books are published by Random House Children's Publishers UK,
61–63 Uxbridge Road, London W5 5SA

www.**randomhousechildrens**.co.uk
www.**totallyrandombooks**.co.uk
www.**randomhouse**.co.uk

Addresses for companies within The Random House Group Limited
can be found at: www.randomhouse.co.uk/offices.htm

THE RANDOM HOUSE GROUP Limited Reg. No. 954009

A CIP catalogue record for this book is available from the British Library.

Printed and bound by CPI Group (UK) Ltd, Croydon, CR0 4YY

THE AUTOBOTS

Optimus Prime

The Autobot leader will stop at nothing to protect Earth.

Bumblebee

Brave and very loyal, Bumblebee communicates with humans by bleeping.

Bulkhead

This Autobot is big, strong and really heavy. Bulkhead is kind of shy, too!

THE AUTOBOTS

Arcee
Arcee fights like a
ninja and her vehicle
mode is a super
speedy motorbike.

Ratchet
The Autobot medic,
Ratchet, is a
techno genius.

Tailgate
Tailgate was Arcee's
loyal partner, until he
lost a battle with
the Cons.

THE DECEPTICONS

Megatron

The evil leader of the Decepticons, Megatron wants to use Dark Energon to conquer Earth.

Starscream

Megatron's second-in-command, Starscream, is sneaky and evil.

Soundwave

A silent spy, Soundwave can tap into and record any kind of electronic transmission.

THE DECEPTICONS

Airachnid
Scary and spider-like, Airachnid is Arcee's arch-enemy.

Knockout
Knockout is the Cons' medic and he is on Starscream's side, always ready to assist in his schemes.

CHAPTER ONE

CRASH LANDING

The black night sky was covered with hundreds of gleaming stars, and a single point of light was moving quickly between them. At first it looked like a dot, no bigger than any other star, but then it seemed to grow larger as it moved closer and closer towards the Earth. It picked up speed as it

disappeared behind the moon, flew out from the other side and then plunged into the atmosphere. It left a long trail of smoke behind as it hurtled across the sky, down to the planet's surface.

It screeched loudly past a snow-covered mountain and over a dark green forest, lighting up the trees as it went. It flew lower before landing with a deafening boom. Trees were thrown aside and the object carved a long, muddy trench into the ground as it shuddered to a halt.

The object was sleek and metallic, and it smoked gently in the cold air of the night. It had landed a long way from any towns, so there *was no one around to hear the low hum of what sounded like an engine deep inside. There was no one around to hear the whirring of a small ramp descending from the base of the object to the forest floor. And there was no one around to hear the tip-tap of metal feet as something nasty scuttled down the ramp and disappeared into the night . . .*

The next day, Arcee and Jack were walking through the same forest, unaware of the events of the previous evening. The air was thick with bugs.

Jack Darby was a fifteen-year-old boy with slick black hair and a friendly face. A few months ago he'd been just a regular kid with a part-time job in a drive-thru restaurant. Then one day he had sat on what he thought was a regular motorbike, only to discover it was actually an Autobot disguised in vehicle mode. Since that day he had been on many adventures with Arcee, but he still felt like he was being treated as someone who needed to be protected rather than as a partner. He wanted to be thought of as a real member of their team!

So when Arcee had asked Jack to come on a 'routine recon' mission, he'd jumped at the chance. Now, as he swatted at several mosquitoes, he was starting to regret it.

'I *really* wish I'd packed some insect repellent,' he complained.

Arcee didn't react. She was walking a short distance ahead, pushing on through the undergrowth of the forest with a determined look on her face.

Jack caught up with her as she stopped to check her hand-held scanner. She was using it to search for Energon, the blue crystals of fuel that she and her Autobot friends used as a power source. She studied the scanner for a moment with her shining blue robotic eyes, before carrying onwards.

Jack squished yet another mosquito

onto his forearm and followed. 'The mosquitoes out here are the size of vampire bats, and they drink just about as much blood!'

Arcee looked down at him. 'You're quite the outdoor guy, aren't you, Jack?' she said with a smile.

'You wouldn't be making fun of my survival kit, would you?' Jack shot back jokingly. 'I may not have sting-proof metal skin, but I can use my multi-function pocket knife and fire-starter to cook up some freeze-dried macaroni and cheese.'

Jack held out his pocket knife for Arcee

to look at, spreading it open to show the various tools it contained. She looked unimpressed though, and held up her Energon scanner. 'You have your tools, I have mine.'

Suddenly the scanner started to bleep. Arcee looked at it, concerned. 'That's odd. Ratchet's satellite scans were accurate, but underground Energon deposits don't cause this kind of surge.'

She held the scanner in front of her and started to follow it towards the source of the disturbance. Jack ran after her as she pushed a path through the undergrowth, and the scanner bleeped rapidly as they got closer to their target.

They soon emerged into a wide clearing in the forest. Jack was surprised to see a large scorch-marked trench cut into the ground in front of them and he thought he could smell smoke in the air. 'What happened here?' he asked.

'A crash landing,' answered Arcee, with a grave look on her face. 'Stay behind me, low and close.'

She bent down low and darted from tree to tree as she followed the path of the trench. Jack ran as fast as he could, struggling to keep up. Arcee was at her fastest in her motorbike vehicle mode, but even in robot mode her legs were almost twice as tall as Jack's entire body. She could move *very* quickly.

Panting and wheezing, Jack caught up with her as she stopped a short distance ahead. Beyond the line of trees lay a compact spaceship, which was still smouldering gently from its journey through space.

'Autobot or Decepticon?' Jack asked.

'Can't tell,' said Arcee. 'Wait here.'

Jack watched as she darted out from behind the trees and ran towards the ship, keeping her body low and her blaster arm raised high.

She spotted a small ramp underneath the ship and ran towards it, aiming her blaster at whatever might be inside, and slowly entered the vessel. A moment later, Jack saw her emerge, but instead of running back to him, she leaned against the ship's hull and stared into space. She was in shock.

'*Arcee?*' called Jack in a hushed voice, but Arcee wasn't listening. She was remembering events that happened a long time ago, back during the war against the Decepticons on Cybertron . . .

Evil, cunning purple eyes shining at her out of the darkness . . .

Large insect-like metal legs scuttling towards her . . .

A claw raised in the darkness, ready to attack . . .

When she didn't respond to Jack's cries, he ran over to her. 'Arcee, what's wrong?'

Slowly, Arcee turned towards him. He had never seen her look more afraid. 'I know who this ship belongs to,' she told him.

CHAPTER TWO

DITCHED IN THE FOREST

Without stopping to explain, Arcee put a finger to her ear to activate her comm-link. 'Arcee to base. I need a GroundBridge ASAP!'

The GroundBridge was a portal that could get them out of this forest to any other place on the planet in an instant, and right now Arcee wanted to be *anywhere* but here.

Jack waved his arms, struggling to get her attention. 'Wait – what's wrong? Whose ship is this?'

Arcee ignored him, and tried the comm-link again. 'Base, do you read me?' she said urgently. 'Scrap! The comm-link is dead. That ship's got to be transmitting a high-frequency scrambler pulse.' She needed to get far enough away from the ship to send her message.

She started to walk off into the forest and Jack followed quickly, pressing her for more information. 'Arcee, you're kind of freaking me out here!'

But Arcee wasn't ready to answer any questions. 'Wait here!' she ordered sternly. She stopped to examine some scratch marks between two trees. Beyond them, a swath of broken branches formed a trail that led off into the forest. Something had been through here. Something *big*.

Suddenly Arcee was flooded with painful memories from the war on Cybertron again, memories that were even more vivid than the ones from before . . .

She remembered being hung from the ceiling in glowing blue stasis cuffs, as a shadowy figure with six arms and two legs scuttled slowly towards her . . .

She remembered struggling as a sharp metal claw extended towards her . . .

Jack could see that his friend was in distress. 'Arcee!' he yelled in desperation, and the shout brought the Autobot back into the present.

She instantly changed into vehicle mode, turning into a sleek blue motorbike. She revved her engines impatiently. 'Climb on!' she ordered.

Still frustrated that she hadn't told him what was going on, Jack put on his motorbike helmet and climbed onto Arcee's back. He barely had time to grab onto the handlebars before she shot off through the trees at incredible speed.

As he held on for his dear life, Jack wondered why they seemed to be riding away from both the spaceship and the tracks leading from it. Whatever had landed here, Arcee wanted to get away from it as quickly as possible.

He squinted against the wind and tried to see where they were headed, before realizing that they were driving straight towards a wide chasm!

'Whoa, Arcee!' called Jack nervously, but she didn't seem to hear him. She accelerated directly towards the edge and Jack screamed as they flew over the chasm and landed on the other side with a bump, before skidding to a stop.

Jack climbed off immediately. 'Was that really necessary?' he complained, but Arcee was trying the comm-link again.

'Arcee to base . . . *Scrap!*' They'd driven

quite a way from the ship, but there was still no signal. It seemed that whatever was happening, she would have to face it by herself.

Jack was angry that Arcee was shutting him out. If he was going to be her partner, then he needed to know what was going on. 'Look, I've seen danger before, so what's the big problem?'

Arcee ignored him. 'Wait here,' she said sternly. 'I *mean* it this time!'

Jack couldn't believe what he was hearing. 'First you shut me out and now you're *ditching* me? I thought I was your partner!'

Arcee switched back into robot mode and stood up tall so as to make her point. 'No, Jack, you're a kid! You're only here because this was supposed to be a "no risk" mission. Got it?'

Without waiting to hear his response, Arcee changed into vehicle mode again and sped back towards the chasm, jumping it easily and racing off into the trees.

Jack was furious. He and Arcee had faced many dangers together since they had met. True, he didn't have any special powers and he wasn't made of metal, but he had helped the Autobots in their battles against the Decepticons. He deserved the right to be treated as a partner, but how could he help Arcee if she kept shutting him out?

Well, he wasn't going to just sit here and wait for her to come and collect him. She might need his help, whether she wanted it or not!

He walked over and looked down into the chasm. There was no way he could jump it by himself, but luckily it wasn't too deep. He'd just have to do this the old-fashioned way. He hauled himself over the edge and started to climb slowly downwards.

CHAPTER THREE

MEMORIES OF CYBERTRON

Arcee sped through the forest as the sun was starting to set. She felt a little guilty about leaving Jack behind, but she knew it was for his own good. What she was about to face was something so terrible that she wanted him as far away from it as possible.

She skidded to a halt when she spotted the trail of broken branches leading away from the spaceship. She switched into robot mode, raised her blaster arm ready to fight, and followed the trail through the trees.

As she walked, a strange glow caught her eye. A broken tree stump was covered with a slimy substance that gave off a ghostly yellow glow. In a flash, she remembered where she had seen the ooze before . . .

Years ago, when the Civil War was still being waged on Cybertron, Arcee had run for her life through a landscape ravaged by war. Explosions echoed all around her. Laser shots rebounded off the rubble and dust filled the air. There was no time to move covertly, she just needed to get out of there as quickly as she could.

'Arcee to Delta Team!' she yelled into her comm-link. 'Requesting rendezvous coordinates. Do you copy?'

The voice of her Autobot partner, Tailgate,

crackled over the comm-link. 'Are you lost again? Your sense of direction could use some improvement.'

Arcee smiled in spite of herself. 'So could your aim, Tailgate. If you'd tagged that sniper back at the artillery depot, I wouldn't have had to break ranks and engage the enemy hand-to-hand.'

The warmth in Tailgate's voice told Arcee that he was just glad to hear she was alive. 'From the sound of things, I'm guessing you came out ahead?' he asked.

'Try waiting for me this time and I'll give you a blow-by-blow account,' she replied. 'What's your position?'

'I'm about half a klick from the depot, due north. Think you can find it, partner?'

'Trust me, Tailgate, my navigation skills are—'

She didn't get to finish the sentence. A web-like net flew out of the darkness and caught her square in the chest, carrying her with it as it pounded into a wall! The net was sticky, and strands of it stuck her firmly to the wall, leaving her unable to move.

Something large with bright shiny purple eyes came at her out of the night. It raised a weapon and fired more of the sticky web at her face, blocking out her vision and knocking her unconscious.

She awoke later in some kind of underground bunker. She could tell that she wasn't injured too badly, but her arms were pinned above her head in stasis cuffs, and more of the sticky web was holding her legs firmly in position. She peered into the darkness and tried to work out where she was.

A mocking voice called out from somewhere behind her, 'If you want my advice, you'll make yourself comfortable.'

A dark shadow appeared from the back of the room. It was a spider-like Decepticon, with six long arms held up high and two shorter legs that allowed it to walk upright. It smiled a sickening smile at her. 'You're going to be here a while.'

The Decepticon reached forward with one of its spindly arms, stretching out a sharp claw on its end, which scratched a shallow wound on Arcee's face. The scratch itself didn't hurt too much, but then it started to burn with some sort of poison and she saw ghostly yellow smoke . . .

Arcee looked down at the yellow smoke rising from the tree stump. As she had feared, her old enemy, Airachnid, had landed

on Earth. The stump was still smoking, so
Arcee knew she must have passed by quite
recently . . .

In a circle of trees not far from there, a
camper was settling down inside his tent. As
he warmed up some soup, he had no idea
that an evil being was watching him silently
from the bushes.

Purple eyes lit up the outside of the tent.
Airachnid activated her tracking vision,
which allowed her to see through the thin
canvas of the tent and secretly study the
human sitting inside. Airachnid smiled. 'My
first "local",' she said to herself with glee.
'Time for humankind to feel my *sting*!'

She then activated her hunt mode, which
extended her six arms and lifted her up
so that she could walk like a spider. She
scuttled towards the tent and raised a sharp
claw, ready to strike . . .

CHAPTER FOUR

AIRACHNID'S TROPHIES

Airachnid leaped into the air and threw herself at the tent. But a split-second before impact, Arcee jumped out of the bushes and slammed into her side! The two of them flew away from the tent and over the edge of a small incline, then rolled over and over before slamming into a rock wall at the bottom of the slope.

Airachnid quickly picked herself up and leaped backwards, landing on eight legs. She took a moment to size up her opponent, and then smiled when she recognized who it was. '*Arcee!* Small universe.'

'Too small, Airachnid,' said Arcee, with fury in her eyes.

Airachnid smiled a sly grin, enjoying Arcee's anger. 'You're still holding a grudge? The war's been over for mega-cycles.'

'Tell that to the Decepticons,' said Arcee, adopting a defensive position as Airachnid started to edge closer.

'My allegiance to Megatron's cause ended eons ago,' replied Airachnid. 'These days I travel solo, in pursuit of my new hobby.'

Arcee grimaced as she remembered what she'd found inside Airachnid's ship earlier that day. Different alien species had been trapped inside green glass cases and were being displayed as a collection.

'Yeah, I saw your souvenir case,' she shot back at Airachnid.

'You mean my *trophies*? Nebulons, Quintessons, Vok . . . I collect endangered species,' she smirked. 'Of course, they aren't really *endangered* until they meet me, but I do the sporting thing and allow them to defend themselves. That way I get to collect their primitive weapons, too. And of course, I have a slot reserved for "human".'

Anger welled up inside Arcee. Airachnid

was a dangerous opponent, but she couldn't allow this evil to go unchecked.

'That's not going to happen,' she warned Airachnid, with a look of determination in her eyes, before leaping at the Decepticon and sending them both tumbling to the ground again.

The two of them rolled over and over in the dirt before Arcee managed to pin Airachnid down and line up a punch to her face. But the blow never landed, as Airachnid kicked out with two of her many legs, knocking Arcee onto her back.

Arcee rolled as she landed and stood up immediately, her blasters raised and ready to fire. She shot lasers towards Airachnid, but the Decepticon was too nimble. She leaped up into the trees to get away, jumping from one branch to another as blasts rebounded all around her.

When she saw a good moment to return fire, Airachnid raised two of her spidery arms and shot some of her super-sticky web directly at Arcee. The webbing was right on target and it wrapped itself tightly around Arcee's arms, trapping them tightly together. However, the string of webbing was still attached to Airachnid, so Arcee yanked on it as hard as she could. The motion pulled Airachnid out of the tree and sent her crashing to the ground with a bump.

While Airachnid was distracted, Arcee tore the webbing from her arms and began firing at her enemy again. Airachnid dodged left and right before raising two spidery blaster arms and firing some shots of her own back at Arcee.

Arcee leaped into the air, grabbed an overhanging tree branch and swung herself round to avoid the blaster fire. When the angle was just right, she let go of the branch and flew through the air, landing a flying kick to Airachnid's chest. The kick pinned Airachnid to the ground and trapped her as Arcee raised her blaster arms and aimed them at her opponent.

Before she could shoot, Arcee heard rocks tumbling down the incline. She looked up and was shocked to see Jack sliding down the slope towards them. The foolish boy must have followed her, after she had warned him not to! And now here he was, the perfect target for Airachnid . . .

'*No!*' she shouted to Jack as a warning, but Airachnid took advantage of the distraction and regained the upper hand by hitting out at Arcee and knocking her backwards.

Arcee staggered, trying to regain her footing, and Airachnid shot an extra-large, extra-sticky web straight at her chest. It sent her flying through the trees, encasing her body and pinning her to the large rock wall behind her. She struggled to get her blasters free, but it was no use. She was trapped!

'Arcee!' shouted Jack, seeing the trouble his friend was in. He ran towards her, wanting to help, but Airachnid was quicker and got there first. She raised herself up, ready to attack Jack!

CHAPTER FIVE

FALLEN PARTNERS

Arcee struggled fiercely in her web restraints, desperate to escape and help her friend. She managed to release one of the blades that popped out of the side of her blaster. It cut through the webbing on one side, freeing her arm just enough

so that she could send a blaster shot directly at Airachnid. It caught her dead on, sending her flying. The Decepticon hit her head against the ground and was knocked out.

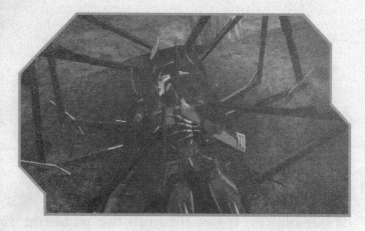

Jack ran up to Arcee. She did *not* look pleased to see him! 'I told you to wait for me!' she scolded.

'Partners don't ditch partners!' Jack shot back in defiance. He started to pull at the sticky webbing, trying to free Arcee.

Arcee wasn't impressed by his outburst. She had almost defeated Airachnid when he had distracted her. 'Jack, you're *not* my partner. And at the moment, you're a liability!'

Jack was stunned. 'I can see it in your eyes. You're afraid, Arcee, and you're never afraid!' he said.

The words hit home. Arcee was more afraid of this enemy than almost anything she could imagine. She grimaced as painful memories came flooding back to her once again . . .

Back in the bunker cell on Cybertron, Airachnid approached the imprisoned Arcee.

'You know, for an Autobot, your resilience is quite impressive. I'm guessing that no matter what I do to you, you'll never crack. Am I right?'

Arcee stared angrily into Airachnid's eyes, but refused to respond. Airachnid was trying to get her to talk about the Autobot attack plans. She didn't know the exact details herself, but if she revealed anything about the plans at all, she could be putting the lives of all her friends at risk. She had to remain silent, no matter how much Airachnid threatened her.

'That's what I thought,' said Airachnid with a smile. It was almost as if she was pleased that Arcee was refusing to talk.

As if on cue, double doors behind Airachnid slid open to reveal two Decepticons carrying the slumped figure of an Autobot. They dragged it towards Arcee, and she squinted to try and make out who it was. A look of horror appeared on her face when she realized it was her combat partner, Tailgate, who she'd been talking to over the comm-link just a short time ago! How had they managed to capture him?

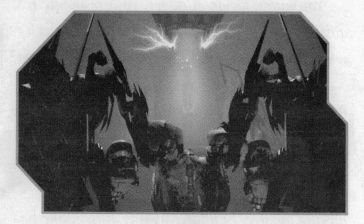

'Tailgate?' she called, but he seemed to be in a bad way and didn't respond. She watched helplessly as the Decepticon soldiers dragged Tailgate across the room and dropped him onto the floor opposite her. They activated another pair of stasis cuffs that lifted him up into the air so he was hanging by his arms. He groaned in pain.

'What have you done to him?' demanded Arcee, with new fury in her voice.

'Not much,' said Airachnid with a grin. 'At least, not much yet. Just tell me what I want to know, or . . . Well, you're a smart Bot. I think you can imagine what happens to Tailgate next.'

'I don't know the attack coordinates!' insisted Arcee. 'I swear upon the AllSpark, it's the truth!'

Airachnid shook her head in disbelief. 'We shall see.' She laughed, then turned and walked slowly towards the limp form of Tailgate, raising two of her spidery legs high into the air.

Arcee struggled against her restraints, desperate to get free and help her friend. 'No! Please!' she begged.

But it was no use. Airachnid raised one of her claws towards Arcee's partner . . .

On that fateful day on Cybertron, many years ago, Arcee had been unable to stop Airachnid from hurting her partner. Now that she was facing Airachnid here on Earth, she was determined not to let the same thing happen again.

'You're right, Jack, I *am* afraid,' she admitted. 'I'm afraid of losing *you*!'

Jack stopped tugging at the webbing around Arcee. He could hear footsteps behind him.

'You really do have trouble hanging onto your partners, don't you?' called Airachnid, who had woken up and was walking slowly towards them. 'We both know what happened to Tailgate, but I recently picked up some Decepticon radio chatter regarding the passing of a Bot called Cliffjumper.'

Arcee grimaced and turned to Jack. 'Don't you get it? She's not interested in *me*! She hunts indigenous species, and she's on Earth so that means *humans*! You! *Run*!'

Jack felt terror bubble up inside his stomach as he realized his mistake. Arcee hadn't been trying to shut him out at all. She'd been trying to protect him from an alien who wanted to hunt him down and put him in a display case!

Giving up on freeing Arcee from her sticky bonds, Jack turned and ran as fast as he could back towards the slope. Arcee struggled to free herself and help him, but Airachnid quickly fired a second round of sticky web to keep her trapped firmly in position.

Airachnid, unconcerned by Jack's slow escape up the hill, laughed as she approached Arcee. 'And that's why I prefer to work alone,' she taunted. 'It's so sad when bad things happen to those close to you. Don't get me wrong, I fully intend to snuff out your spark, but that won't compare to the pain you'll feel knowing I'm adding *your* human to my collection!' And with that, she set off in pursuit of Jack, who was still only halfway up the slope.

One teenage boy against a giant, eight-legged Decepticon. He didn't stand a chance. '*Jack!*' shouted Arcee.

CHAPTER SIX

KEEP DRIVING!

Jack was already panting by the time
he reached the top of the slope. He ran
away through the trees as fast as he could,
chancing a look over his shoulder. He
couldn't see Airachnid anywhere. Was
there a chance that Arcee had freed herself
and given him the opportunity to escape?
But then he saw the dark shadow of eight
spidery legs crawl over the edge of the
slope. Evil purple eyes shone at him in the
moonlight.

'That's the spirit, Jack!' called Airachnid.
'Play hard to get!'

★

Down below, Arcee fought desperately to free herself. She couldn't believe she was about to lose another partner. At least the others had had a chance of defending themselves, but Jack was just a human. She had to find a way to help him, somehow. As she struggled, she fought back the memory of that terrible day on Cybertron . . .

Arcee hung miserably in her stasis cuffs. She had given up the struggle and was no longer attempting to escape.

Airachnid was surprised that she hadn't told her the attack coordinates. Maybe she was tougher than she looked, or maybe she really didn't know them after all? Either way, Airachnid had resigned herself to the fact that Arcee wasn't going to tell her anything useful. All that remained now was to dispose of her. She raised a spidery leg, extended a sharp claw and started to move towards Arcee, ready to finish the job . . .

Suddenly a loud explosion rocked the bunker and the double doors behind Airachnid flew open. The Decepticon turned to see two Autobots standing in the smoking wreckage of the doorway, their blasters raised high. She hissed in anger and fired a few shots at them, before leaping towards a different exit and making her escape.

Arcee looked up at the two Autobots standing in the doorway. It was Cliffjumper and Bumblebee. Bumblebee fired shots at the two Decepticon guards, and they instantly fell to the floor.

Cliffjumper ran over and released Arcee from her stasis cuffs, while Bumblebee went to where Tailgate was hanging. Arcee saw him shake his head sadly. They were too late.

'I couldn't save him!' wailed Arcee as they

carried her out of the bunker. 'I couldn't save my partner!'

Back in the forest, Arcee gave up her struggle. The webbing was just too sticky for her to escape from. She hadn't been able to save Tailgate or Cliffjumper, and now she had let down Jack as well.

'Jack, I'm sorry,' she whispered to herself. 'I never should have looked back. I should have—' She stopped suddenly as an idea formed in her mind. 'I should have kept *driving*!' she exclaimed.

She pulled herself as far forward in the web as she could, opening up just enough space between her and the rock to switch into vehicle mode. Her motorbike form was still trapped by the web, but it might just be powerful enough to help her escape . . .

Jack vaulted over a fallen tree trunk that was blocking his path. As he dropped onto the other side, he stumbled to the ground, panting furiously and trying to catch his breath. He couldn't go on running like this for much longer.

Well, if he couldn't *run*, then he would have to *hide*. He pulled himself into a gap under the fallen tree trunk and tried to keep his breathing as quiet as possible. He listened carefully for the sounds of Airachnid's approach.

Jack jumped when he heard a distant scream from somewhere amongst the trees. It took him a moment to realize it was just a bird's cry, and the forest fell silent again. Maybe he'd managed to escape from his pursuer? But then he heard soft metallic footsteps edging closer and closer.

Airachnid crept up behind the fallen tree trunk, scanning the area carefully. She knew Jack must have come this way, but where was he now? She hissed in frustration and leaned over the top of the trunk, searching for her prey.

Directly beneath her, Jack held his breath and tucked his body in as tightly against the tree as he could. Airachnid placed a long spidery leg directly in front of him, then another and another, as she stepped gently over the trunk and started to move away from him into the clearing. Jack breathed

a sigh of relief. She didn't seem to have spotted him.

But then his heart skipped a beat as Airachnid stopped dead. She bent her head upside-down between her legs, and two vicious purple eyes stared directly at him. 'Hello, Jack!'

She had him cornered against the trunk! He stood up and leaped aside as a sharp leg came down towards him. He then turned and vaulted back over the tree trunk, just in time to avoid another swipe.

His legs were exhausted, but he had to keep running. Airachnid hissed in delight. It was time to catch her prey. She shot a ball of sticky web at him, but at the last moment Jack jumped aside and it smacked uselessly into a tree. He ran as fast as he could, knowing that the next ball of web was unlikely to miss . . .

Arcee's motorbike form roared as she revved the engines as hard as she could. The tyres squealed against the floor as the bike slid uselessly from side to side in the mud, still straining to escape from the sticky web.

But slowly, ever so slowly, she felt the web start to weaken and several strands snapped away from the rock. She yelled out with the strain, and with one final big rev of her engine, she was suddenly free!

She raced away through the trees in pursuit of Airachnid and Jack, just hoping she wasn't too late . . .

CHAPTER SEVEN

JACK'S SURVIVAL KIT

Jack darted left and right, trying to stick to places where the trees were closest together, in an attempt to prevent Airachnid from following him through the narrow gaps. Running in this manner had bought him a little time, but he knew he couldn't outrun Airachnid for ever.

He looked from side to side, searching desperately for a new hiding spot. He had to stop suddenly when he came across another chasm in the forest floor. With a grunt of frustration, he realized that it was too wide to jump over. If he accidentally fell, he certainly wouldn't be able to escape from Airachnid with a broken leg.

So, as quickly and as carefully as he could, he lowered himself over the edge and started to climb down. He soon reached the bottom, then clambered across the base of the chasm and pulled himself up the other side.

But negotiating the chasm had wasted valuable seconds, and when he looked back he was horrified to see that Airachnid had caught up and was approaching swiftly from the other side! Jack turned and ran.

Airachnid stopped to size up the gap. It might be too wide for a teenage boy to jump, but it would be no problem for a Decepticon. She leaned back on her eight legs and, with one graceful leap, she sprang across the chasm and landed easily on the other side, just a short way behind Jack.

Jack ran through the trees, dodging this way and that, still searching for a good hiding spot. His lungs screamed at him and he knew he had to slow down or he would collapse into a heap. He jumped behind a large tree and leaned against it, trying to get his breath back. If he was going to survive this, he needed to come up with a plan.

Hmm, he thought to himself. *My 'survival kit' might be able to help*. He reached down into his pocket and took out his multi-function pocket knife. He spread it open and cycled through the various tools.

A can opener . . .

A corkscrew . . .

A nail-file . . .

A *fish descaler* . . . ?

There were several other implements that he didn't recognize, but somehow none of them looked like they were designed for destroying giant Decepticon spiders from outer space. It was hopeless. 'Who am I kidding?' he asked himself.

He saw movement out of the corner of his eye and realized that Airachnid had found him again. He stumbled into a run, wondering how much further he could possibly hope to get.

Airachnid was starting to tire of the chase, too. She had simply been toying with him so far, in the hope that he would put up more of a fight. If this was the best that human opponents could do, then she was very disappointed.

'You're making this too easy, Jack,' she called, 'and I do not enjoy being *bored*!'

Jack stumbled over a ledge and emerged into a wide clearing. With a start, he realized he was standing back in the trench that had been carved by Airachnid's ship when it landed. He looked up to see the moon reflecting off the hull of her ship. This could be the one place in the whole forest where she wouldn't expect him to hide.

He stumbled down the hill towards the ship. Maybe he could find some alien weapons inside that would help him fight Airachnid? As he cast a look back over his shoulder, he saw her appear from between the trees and stand up tall to survey the scene.

He darted quickly behind one of the tall metal supports for the ship's landing ramp. Had she seen him? If he went inside and Airachnid noticed him, he would be trapped in there. So he stayed where he was, waiting to see where she would go next.

Airachnid studied the landing site. There was no sign of Jack. 'Where did you scamper off to?' she called.

In one graceful bound, she leaped onto the top of the ship and scuttled along the roof towards the landing ramp. When she got to the end, she jumped up in the air and spun round, landing on the ramp in front of the open entrance.

'If you wanted a tour, Jack, all you had to do was ask!' She approached the entrance slowly. 'Did you spot the empty case? It's the one I've reserved for you.'

As she disappeared inside, Jack breathed a sigh of relief. He had made the right decision not to hide inside the ship. It would probably take Airachnid a minute or two to search the place, and that would buy him some valuable time. Staying low and silent, he darted from his hiding spot and ran behind the ship.

He stopped as he stepped in something sticky and wet. A pool of dark blue liquid was forming a puddle on the ground. He followed the path of the liquid and saw that it was dripping down from inside the ship's enormous exhaust pipes.

'Energon!' exclaimed Jack, recognizing the fuel that powered not only the Autobots and the Decepticons, but also their spaceships. *And fuel burns*, he thought, coming up with a plan. *Looks like my survival kit might come in useful after all . . .*

He picked up a piece of scrap metal that had broken off the spaceship and pulled out his multi-function pocket knife. He rubbed the blade of his knife along the piece of metal, and yellow sparks flew into the air.

Inside the ship, Airachnid's super-sensitive hearing picked the scraping of Jack's knife. 'Jack?' she called, quickly setting out after the source of the noise.

Jack scraped harder, bending down to aim the sparks towards a piece of tree branch, and soon it was smoking nicely. He picked it up carefully and blew on it to feed the fire with oxygen, and the smoke kindled into a bright orange flame.

He knew his aim had to be perfect. Drawing back his arm, he threw the flaming branch up into the air towards the ship's exhaust pipe. Even as it left his hand, he knew it would be on target.

Jack turned to run just as Airachnid reappeared on top of her ship. She saw him fleeing towards the trees, and then spotted the fiery branch flying through the air. It landed inside the exhaust pipe with a *plop*, right in the middle of the Energon pool, and the flames started to spread quickly.

Too late, Airachnid realized what he had done. '*Jack!*' she screamed, but her cry was cut off as an almighty BOOM sounded across the clearing. The Energon had exploded!

CHAPTER EIGHT

SO MUCH FOR CLOSURE

Jack could feel the heat on the back of his neck as a series of explosions blew Airachnid's ship sky-high. The power of one of the blasts knocked him off his feet, and sent him flying through the trees. He landed with a bump, then turned over and shielded his eyes against the bright light of the fire.

After a moment, he pulled himself up onto his feet. Relief washed over him as he watched the smoking wreckage of Airachnid's ship. Nothing could have survived an explosion that big! He had actually beaten a Decepticon all by himself!

He turned and started to walk away through the trees in search of Arcee. Just wait until she heard about *this*!

Suddenly, something whistled through the air and landed with a *snap* on his left foot. He looked down. It was a piece of Airachnid's sticky web, and it had stuck his foot firmly to the ground.

He looked up into the trees, in the direction the web had flown from. The still-flaming figure of Airachnid loomed above him. She was clearly damaged, but she was still alive!

She quickly fired another shot of web, which knocked him back and stuck him against a tree. Airachnid grinned in triumph. The human had shown great cunning and had actually put up a decent fight in the end, but she had caught him all the same!

She clambered down and approached her prey with a wild fury in her eyes. She reached out her claws and brushed them gently against Jack's face. She wasn't happy about what he'd done to her ship . . .

The roar of an engine distracted her. She looked up and saw a motorbike racing towards them through the clearing. It flew up a ridge and jumped, switching back into robot mode in the air and throwing a punch that Airachnid was completely unprepared for.

She landed with a bump, and before she even had time to get to her feet, Arcee was on top of her. The Bot attacked with a series of kicks and punches that Airachnid was too dazed to even defend herself against. With one final, powerful kick, Arcee sent her enemy flying away through the air.

Airachnid knocked several trees out of the way with the force of her flight, before landing in a crumpled heap, dazed and defeated. She wouldn't be getting up any time soon.

Arcee turned to Jack. 'Are you OK?' she asked, pulling away the webbing that was sticking him to the tree.

Jack felt himself all over. He had a few bumps and scrapes, but he wasn't seriously injured. He smiled at Arcee. 'Yeah, of course,' he said, and held up his pocket knife in triumph. 'Survival kit!'

Arcee smiled, but the smile quickly dropped from her face when she heard a furious drilling sound coming from behind her. She turned and saw Airachnid, standing up and drilling down into the ground. She was trying to escape!

Arcee fired a few blaster shots, but

Airachnid had already jumped into the hole. She ran over to see a long tunnel disappearing into the ground.

'*Airachnid*!' she screamed in anger, but her enemy was already long gone. Who knew where and when she would pop up again? Arcee sighed in frustration. 'So much for closure.'

Jack came up behind her and looked down into the hole. 'Now Airachnid's stuck here on Earth,' he realized. 'I'm not sure that's such a good thing.'

Arcee turned to Jack. She would worry about Airachnid another day. For now, she was concerned about having let her friend down. 'I'm sorry you had to face my demons today,' she said, then smiled. 'You were pretty fearless there, Jack.'

Jack beamed at the compliment, but he couldn't ignore the truth of what had really happened. 'Actually, I was terrified. Mostly for you.'

Arcee smiled. It was time to go home.

With Airachnid's ship destroyed, the scrambler pulse would have been deactivated, so Arcee should finally be able to contact base. She put a finger to her ear to activate her comm-link. 'Ratchet, this is Arcee requesting a GroundBridge.' The comm-link beeped in acknowledgement.

An irritating buzzing noise distracted Jack, and he swatted a mosquito out of the air. Arcee smiled, and spoke into the comm-link: 'I need to get my partner away from any over-sized insects.'

Jack looked up and grinned when he realized what she had said. 'Partner, huh?'

'*Junior* partner!' corrected Arcee. 'I can still pull rank.'

The two partners laughed as a glowing GroundBridge portal opened up to carry them home.

TRANS FORMERS

P R I M E

MIND GAMES

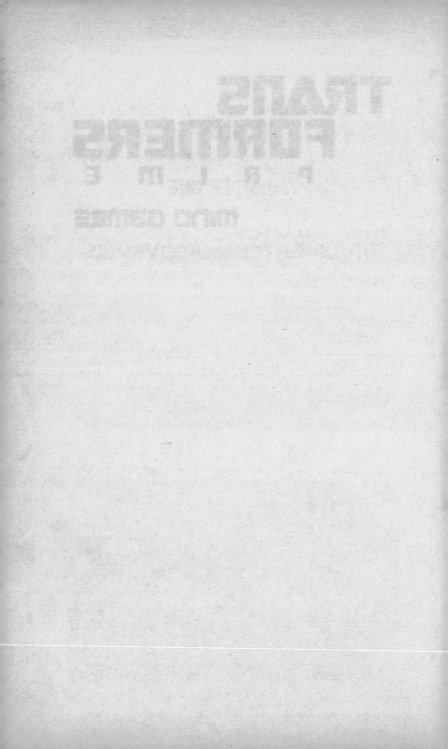

CHAPTER ONE

UNEXPECTED DISCOVERIES

Deep inside Autobot Outpost Omega
One, which was located under a mountain
in the Nevada desert, Ratchet was staring
at his monitor screen in amazement.
'Optimus,' he called, 'you're not going to
believe this . . .'

As the Autobots' medic, Ratchet was responsible for patching up the Autobots after their many battles with the evil Decepticons. But he was a technical genius, too, looking after their advanced computer systems and helping them search for deposits of Energon.

He had been running various scans when he had discovered something almost too good to be true. Optimus Prime, the leader of the Autobots, walked up behind Ratchet to look at the monitor screen. It showed a bright green map of planet Earth. Some red dotted lines encircled a red box that was flashing over a location in Eastern Asia.

Optimus wondered if Ratchet had located another source of Energon, which both the Autobots and Decepticons used as a source of fuel, but Ratchet had actually found something even more exciting than that.

'I've just pinpointed the location of

the Decepticon warship!' said Ratchet.

Optimus couldn't believe what he was hearing. The Autobots were dedicated to protecting the people of Earth from the evil of the Decepticons, but their enemies were very good at remaining hidden. Their leader, Megatron, had been killed in a Spacebridge explosion some time ago, but Optimus knew that the Cons still posed a threat. Locating their warship was an unexpected and lucky surprise.

'How did you penetrate their cloaking technology?' he asked.

'I didn't,' explained Ratchet. 'I was experimenting with variable frequency wavelengths when I stumbled upon it. Their ship must be experiencing some kind of electro-magnetic breach.'

The other Autobots were listening carefully to the news. Arcee didn't really care *how* they had found the Decepticons' warship; all she was interested in was taking advantage of the news while they could. She turned to her friends, Bulkhead and Bumblebee, and could see the same mixture of worry and excitement on their faces. She made a fist. 'With Megatron deceased and the element of surprise . . .'

'We could do some *serious* damage!' said Bulkhead, finishing her sentence for her.

Optimus considered his options. As leader of the Autobots, he knew he must never lead his friends into battle unless it was absolutely necessary. Although he wasn't unused to firing the first shot in any fight, he felt uneasy about going on the offensive without more information. But he knew only too well how much damage the Decepticons had already caused to the people of Earth. Could this finally be the Autobots' chance to end their long battle, once and for all?

A series of loud beeps from the monitor screen grabbed his attention. A blue box had appeared on the map, some way south of the location of the Decepticon warship.

Ratchet explained what it was. 'It's an Autobot emergency beacon, also on the same frequency.'

A distress signal was an important matter, and it overrode any other considerations for now. 'The Decepticons can wait,' ordered Optimus. 'There may be Autobots in distress. Ratchet, bring your medical kit.'

Ratchet tapped at his controls,

activating the GroundBridge that would take them to the location of the distress signal. Across the hangar, a swirling blue-green portal opened up. Optimus and Ratchet walked calmly into the portal, and a moment later emerged on the other side of the planet.

It had been daytime back at the Autobot base, but over here it was night. The moonlight revealed the rusty wreckage of an Autobot spaceship. It was half buried in the desert, and Optimus got the sense that it was much larger than it appeared from the small portion he could see.

'A crash landing, buried here for centuries,' said Optimus.

'The shifting sand must have finally unearthed it, which explains why we've only just picked up the emergency beacon,' Ratchet added.

They surveyed the ship, wondering if there were any Autobots still alive inside. 'If they travelled in stasis mode, there may be survivors,' the medic Bot observed.

They approached the ship and when they were close enough, Optimus used his blaster arm to cut a hole in the side of the hull; stale air flowed out. They looked in and realized the ship must have crashed upside down, as they could see light fittings by their feet. Optimus and Ratchet stepped carefully through the gap, their combined weight making the ship shift slightly in the sand.

The two Autobots steadied themselves as the ship settled, then activated torches in their hands and shone them up and down the corridor. Optimus recognized

the ship type. It was a Vanguard–class Deep Space Transport, which would have carried refugees from the Great War on Cybertron rather than warriors.

They carefully made their way to the end of the corridor, stopping once or twice to keep their balance as the ship shifted in the sand. At the end of the corridor, an automatic hatchway barred their entrance onto the bridge of the ship. With no electric power to activate the hatch, Optimus wrenched the door open by hand with a loud *screech!* The air that wafted through the doorway carried the scent of rust and oil.

As they stepped into the room, Optimus' torch revealed a horrible sight. Three broken Autobots lay on the floor in pools of Energon. They were rusty and their sparks had clearly diminished a long time ago. Optimus shook his head sadly. *They are at one with the AllSpark*, he thought to himself.

Ratchet bent down over one of the Autobots and ran his forearm scanner over its body. A look of fear crossed his face as he read the results. 'Optimus, these Autobots didn't perish in the crash. They're displaying the effects of a virus!'

'This is a plague ship,' said Optimus gravely. In which case there would be no survivors. 'I must activate the self-destruct sequence,' he decided, with regret.

He took a step towards the controls, but Ratchet held out a hand to stop him, just before he stood in a puddle of infected Energon. 'Don't touch anything!' cautioned Ratchet. 'The virus may still be active.'

Suddenly the unstable ship lurched to one side, sending Optimus and Ratchet flying into a wall. As they climbed back onto their feet, Optimus heard a creaking sound from high above his head. He looked up to see another departed

Autobot, still strapped into the pilot's seat on the floor high above him. The movement of the ship had jostled the pilot about in his seat and set loose a single droplet of infected Energon, which fell through the air . . .

'*No!*' screamed Ratchet as he realized what was about to happen. But he was too late. The tiny drop of Energon landed directly in Optimus' eye. He had been infected with the virus!

CHAPTER TWO

THE SEARCH FOR A CURE

The effects of the virus set in almost immediately. Optimus stumbled, and Ratchet leaped in to offer his support. He quickly activated the ship's self-destruct, and then helped Optimus to climb back out through the hull and onto the sand.

He activated his comm-link and spoke in an urgent tone. 'Arcee, prepare a level-five decontamination screen!' He couldn't quite bring himself to tell them what had happened. 'We have an Autobot in distress . . .'

Together they stumbled away from

the ship as the blue-green swirl of the GroundBridge opened up ahead. Ratchet helped Optimus into the portal just in time, before the ship exploded behind them with a *bang*. At least now nobody else would be infected.

In the sick bay of the Autobot base, Optimus was lying down on a bed while Ratchet ran medical scans on him. Already the medic Bot could see a worrying patch of rusty brown infection spreading across his friend's face, and the lights of his eyes were flickering in an unsettling manner.

Ratchet used a hand-held medical analyser to scan Optimus. He shook his head sadly when he saw the results. 'Cybonic plague,' he said grimly. It was exactly as he'd feared.

He turned to look at the rest of the team. Bumblebee, Arcee and Bulkhead stood in a half-circle, expressions of worry on their faces. They were concerned for their friend, but they also feared they might become infected themselves.

Ratchet reassured them. 'It's only contagious if contact is made with the infected Energon, as happened with Optimus.' He was angry with himself. *If only I had reacted more quickly, maybe I could have saved him!* he thought.

From a metal walkway, the three teenagers, Jack, Miko and Raf, were also watching.

'What was a "plague" doing in an Autobot spaceship?' asked Miko, a fourteen-year-old girl who usually hung around with Bulkhead.

Arcee explained, 'Its passengers were infected. The virus wiped out millions on Cybertron during the Great War.'

'Cybonic plague was engineered in the Decepticons' biological warfare programme,' continued Ratchet. 'It was created by Megatron himself.'

Twelve-year-old Raf looked down at Optimus with sad eyes. 'You have a cure though don't you?'

Ratchet couldn't quite bring himself to say the answer out loud. Optimus spoke up in a gravelly voice, to give the answer for him. '*No . . . cure . . .*' he gasped.

'Optimus, please save your strength!' insisted Ratchet.

Jack wasn't buying this. 'Would Megatron really create a disease without having a cure? I mean, what if *he'd* caught it by accident?'

Miko and Raf nodded in agreement, but Bulkhead shook his head wearily, thinking back to the Spacebridge explosion. 'It's not like we can ask Megatron. He's pushing up lugnuts.'

Ratchet had an idea. 'But we might be able to access the Decepticon database!' He turned towards his monitor screen, which was still showing a green map of the world with a red flashing box over the location of the Decepticon warship, the *Nemesis*.

'For the moment, we still have a fix on their warship's location,' he said.

That was all Arcee needed to hear. If

there was the slightest chance that there was a cure for Cybonic plague somewhere on board the *Nemesis*, then Arcee was going to find it. 'Bumblebee, come with me!' she instructed, turning towards the entrance to the GroundBridge. There was no time to lose.

'What about me?' asked Bulkhead. If they were going to help Optimus, he wanted to be a part of it.

Arcee looked up at Bulkhead. Even for an Autobot, he was enormous. 'Sorry, Bulkhead, but you're not exactly built for stealth!' she said.

Ratchet activated the GroundBridge and a swirling blue-green portal appeared. Arcee stepped inside, and Bumblebee followed close behind her.

'Quickly!' Ratchet called after them as the GroundBridge snapped shut.

On the other side of the planet, the Decepticon's warship, the *Nemesis*, was prowling through the night sky. A darkened corridor deep inside the ship was suddenly lit up with blue-green light as the exit to the GroundBridge opened up. Arcee and Bumblebee leaped out of the portal as it closed, their blasters raised and ready for action.

The two Autobots had no way of knowing if they were going to arrive in a room full of Decepticon guards, but luckily the coast appeared to be clear.

'Let's start with the lab,' said Arcee, and together they moved quickly and quietly along the corridor.

It took some careful searching, but after a while they arrived at the entrance to the lab. Suddenly the door whirred open. Arcee and Bumblebee quickly ducked down into an alcove to avoid being seen as a Decepticon emerged into the corridor. It was Knockout, the Decepticons' medic. He turned and strode along the corridor, heading directly towards them!

CHAPTER THREE

THE PATIENT IN THE LAB

Arcee and Bumblebee pressed themselves as far into their alcove as they could while Knockout moved closer and closer. When he reached their location, Knockout stopped dead, a look of concern on his face. Had he sensed that they were there? But then he shrugged, and continued on his way down the corridor.

Not wasting a moment, Arcee and Bumblebee went straight through the open door of the lab, sealing it shut behind them.

The room was large and dark, with numerous alcoves that were filled with all kinds of strange devices and terminals. It was empty now, but it would usually be used as the Decepticons' sick bay. To Arcee it looked like a mad scientist's laboratory.

Bumblebee explored the room while Arcee grabbed the nearest computer terminal and started tapping away at the keyboard. Optimus needed their help quickly, but Arcee also wanted to get off the ship before anyone realized they were there.

The terminal beeped loudly as she

hacked into the system. 'I'm in the network,' she said into her comm-link. 'Searching the files now.'

★

Back at the Autobot base, Ratchet was still in the sick bay keeping a close eye on Optimus' vital signs. He seemed to be stable for now, but he knew there wasn't much time to find a cure.

'*Ratchet . . .*' called Optimus in a weak voice. Every word sounded like it was causing him difficulty. '*Were . . . you . . .*'

'Infected?' said Ratchet, finishing Optimus' sentence for him. 'No, I wasn't.' Ratchet could see a moment of relief through the pain written on Optimus' face.

'*Not . . . much . . . time . . . to . . . select . . . new . . . leader . . .*' gasped Optimus.

Ratchet wasn't prepared to have this discussion. 'You're not leaving us, Optimus. Not with your physician on watch. Now lie back and rest.' Optimus lay back and closed his eyes.

Arcee's voice crackled over the comm-link again. 'If it's here, I don't see it,' she said in frustration.

'Are you *certain*, Arcee?'

'I've searched every file. There's nothing.'

'Well, search again!' snapped the medic Bot, angrily. This was their only chance, and he wasn't prepared to give up that easily. 'Clearly you missed something!'

'I've scanned the entire database!'

While Arcee and Ratchet argued, Bumblebee was still exploring the lab. He looked into a small room at the back of the lab and saw something he couldn't believe. He bleeped loudly to attract Arcee's attention, but she wasn't listening.

'Did you use a redundant quantum algorithm?' asked Ratchet.

'Don't tell me how to research! Do you think you're the only one who cares about Optimus?'

Bumblebee let out a very loud and insistent *BLEEP*!

'What is it, Bumblebee?' snapped Arcee as she walked over to him. She gasped in shock when she saw what Bumblebee had found. Through a glass door in the side of the lab was a giant slab, on which lay a large and unconscious Decepticon. It was the Con leader, Megatron!

'What is it?' called Ratchet over the comm–link. 'What's going on?'

'It's Megatron,' said Arcee, in a state of shock. 'He's alive!'

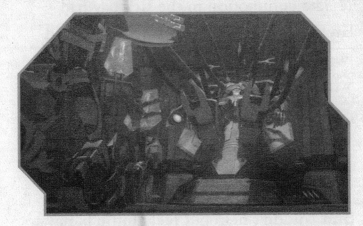

Back at the base, the listening Autobots gasped with shock. 'That's not possible!' said Ratchet.

'Well, I'm *staring* right at him!' said Arcee. Bumblebee bleeped as if to say, *Me too!*

Arcee looked over at the fallen leader of the Decepticons. His eyes were shut and he wasn't moving.

'The good news is that Megatron isn't exactly staring back.' She could see a large tube connecting his spark chamber to a bleeping life-support machine. Arcee realized that he must be in a coma, and that this machine was keeping him alive.

The commotion in the sick bay had awoken Optimus. '*Mega . . . tron?*' he said weakly.

Arcee continued her report. 'He's critical, hooked up to life-support.' She thought of all the trouble he and his Decepticons had caused, including the war on Cybertron and the attacks on Earth, and couldn't help but feel a little happy to see him in this state.

Yet she knew it wasn't enough. So long as he was alive, there was a chance he could start all over again, and she couldn't let that happen. She held up her blaster and pointed it at Megatron with a look of determination on her face. 'Time to finish this, once and for all.'

Ratchet shouted at her over the comm-link, 'Wait! Don't!'

'One good reason. *Fast.*'

'Megatron may be Optimus' only hope of survival!' said Ratchet.

Arcee deactivated her blaster. 'What are you talking about?'

'Does he display brainwave activity?'

Arcee looked up at a life-support monitor that was hanging beside Megatron's bed. A wavy red line displayed his brainwave activity, and it was moving up and down rapidly.

'It's spiking hard,' said Arcee. 'His sick mind is still at work.'

Ratchet was pleased. '*Perfect!* If a cure does exist, Megatron may be the only one who knows it. You must enter his brain and find it, urgently!'

CHAPTER FOUR

a DANGEROUS MISSION

'Enter Megatron's brain?' screamed Arcee.
'Are you out of *your* mind?'

Ratchet explained himself. 'The
Decepticon laboratory should contain all
the equipment you need for a Cortical-
Psychic patch.'

Arcee couldn't believe what she
was hearing. A Cortical-Psychic patch
would allow one of them to go inside
Megatron's brain and search for the
information they needed, but it was
extremely dangerous.

'Have you ever performed this
procedure?' she asked.

'No,' replied Ratchet, 'but I have studied the theoretical literature. The technique was invented by Decepticons and outlawed by the Autobots.'

Arcee desperately tried to think of an alternative. 'Can't we just haul Megatron through the GroundBridge? It'll buy us some time to figure this out.'

'*Time* is one thing that Optimus does not have!' said Ratchet impatiently. 'One of you must try this procedure. I will *not* allow Optimus to pass knowing that Megatron will outlive him!'

Arcee paced up and down. She would do almost anything for Optimus, but this was pushing it. 'Ratchet, I would lay down my life for Optimus, anytime, anywhere. But a mind–body split—'

Bumblebee cut her off with a loud and determined *bleep*. Arcee understood what he meant. He was volunteering to go into Megatron's mind.

'You will?' she asked.

Back in the lab, Raf, who was a close friend of Bumblebee's, was worried. 'Are you sure this is safe, Bumblebee?'

Bulkhead tried to reassure Raf. 'Bumblebee is the best scout there is. If anyone can find the cure in there, it's him.'

Raf nodded, but he feared for his friend. Going into the mind of a being as evil as Megatron seemed like a very dangerous idea. Jack and Miko put their arms around Raf's shoulders and comforted him.

On the bridge of the warship *Nemesis*, the

current Decepticon leader, Starscream, was glaring at one of his troopers.

'Why has the electromagnetic shielding not been repaired?' he demanded. He knew that so long as the shields were down, it would be impossible to hide their position, and that meant the Autobots would be able to find them.

'The crews are working as quickly as they can, Lord Starscream,' the trooper replied nervously.

'We are *leaking a trail*!' Starscream yelled. 'All the Autobots need to do to pinpoint our position is access the correct frequency wavelength! Accelerate your efforts!'

'Yes, Lord Starscream!' said the trooper, rushing away quickly.

As he exited the bridge, Knockout entered. 'Doctor in the house!' he called boastfully.

'Ah, Knockout, and how is the patient doing today?' asked Starscream, wondering about Megatron's condition.

Knockout shook his head. 'Same-old, same-old.'

Starscream couldn't help but smile. So long as Megatron was out of the picture, no one would challenge his command of the Decepticons. However, if he wanted complete control over them, he would need to make sure that there was no chance of Megatron ever coming back.

'An inglorious fate that he should remain in this vegetative state!' said Starscream with mock pity.

'On the contrary. Megatron's body may

be scrap metal, but his *mind* is still smokin'!' replied Knockout.

Starscream looked around nervously, making sure they weren't being overheard. '*Keep that to yourself!*' he hissed. 'That blasted Soundwave sees and hears everything!'

Knockout nodded in understanding. 'He's the eyes and ears of the Decepticons.'

Starscream nodded. While he longed for control of the Decepticons, he had to be careful that he didn't trust the wrong person. Many of the Cons still remained loyal to Megatron. Soundwave was one of them, and he would be the most difficult person to persuade that Megatron was gone for good. Starscream knew that he could trust Knockout, however.

'Well, as long as their master remains in limbo, so does their cause,' he said slyly. 'The Decepticons deserve a strong, *alert* leader!'

Knockout smiled, imagining where he

might fit into this plan. 'A leader who would require a loyal second-in-command,' he replied.

Starscream looked at Knockout through narrowed eyes and chuckled. He knew the medic was talking about himself, but first they would need to convince the others that Megatron wasn't going to wake up anytime soon. 'A candidate would need to *earn* that post by making a strong case to said "eyes and ears",' he remarked.

Knockout nodded in understanding. 'A case for showing *mercy*, Lord Starscream?'

Starscream nodded. They understood

each other. Far from showing mercy, they would need to convince Soundwave to let them pull the plug and be rid of Megatron, once and for all!

'You scratch my back,' said Starscream with a smile, 'I scratch yours.' He placed a hand on Knockout's arm.

Knockout smiled, but then took a step back, examining his arm. 'Just don't scratch the paint!' he said.

CHAPTER FIVE

INSIDE MEGATRON'S MIND

Back in the Decepticons' lab, Arcee was
connecting a long cable into the back
of Megatron's brain. Through this, she
would connect Megatron to Bumblebee,
allowing the Autobot to go deep inside the
Decepticon leader's mind.

She reeled the cable out along the floor and down to a hidden area behind Megatron's sick bed, where Bumblebee was lying on an exam table. They needed a safe spot in case anyone came in unexpectedly. She hooked the cable up to a monitor next to Bumblebee. Once the cables were all connected, Arcee spoke into her comm-link. 'Ratchet, we're ready.'

Ratchet was still listening in from the Autobot base, and he nodded. He knew what they were about to attempt was very risky, but he also knew they had no choice.

If there was a chance of saving Optimus, they had to take it. 'Initiate the Cortical-Psychic patch,' he ordered.

On hearing these words, Bumblebee smiled bravely, then gave a thumbs-up and bleeped to show that he was ready to go. Arcee took a final length of cable and plunged it into the back of Bee's head.

Instantly, the Decepticon lab disappeared, and Bumblebee found himself all alone in a black void. In the distance, a single point of light was rushing towards him. As he reached it, it turned into a whirling tunnel and he flew along it faster and faster . . .

And then, all at once, he was standing on solid ground. Where was he? He looked down at his body. He looked exactly like he always did, but Bumblebee knew this wasn't his real body. This was only an avatar, an imaginary projection of his body that he could use to walk around inside Megatron's mind. As his eyes adjusted to the new surroundings, he looked up into a vision of hell.

It was a large Decepticon city that had been torn apart by war. Half-ruined buildings looked ready to fall at any moment and the entire place was glowing red from the numerous fires dotting the horizon. Pools of molten metal flowed across the landscape. Bumblebee remembered this place, but he wished he didn't ...

Back in the Autobot lab, the gang gathered around a monitor that Ratchet was trying to get to work. Suddenly it flickered on.

'Communications downlink activated,' he said. 'This will allow us to see and hear everything Bumblebee does while inside Megatron's subconscious mind.'

Bulkhead and the teens looked at the monitor in awe. They could see the same hellish landscape that Bumblebee was witnessing, as if they were looking through his eyes.

Jack didn't think that Megatron's mind looked like a good place for a holiday. 'Whoa, where is that?' he asked.

Bumblebee bleeped over the comm-link to explain what he was looking at.

'Bee says it looks like Kaon,' Raf translated for the others, 'the Decepticon capital back on Cybertron!'

Below them, Ratchet was checking Optimus' vital signs. They were growing weaker and the colour was starting to drain from his body, leaving him a dull shade of grey. They needed to move quickly.

Ratchet addressed Bumblebee over the comm-link. 'Quickly, Bumblebee. I know you're in unknown territory, but you must figure out where information might be "filed" in Megatron's mind.'

Bumblebee bleeped to show he understood. Somehow, he thought that was probably going to be easier said than done . . .

He crossed a narrow bridge that led into the heart of Kaon, and found himself in a large central plaza surrounded by enormous statues of Megatron. Some of them showed him in the midst of battle, while others simply showed him standing proudly.

Bumblebee moved slowly, worried about what, or who, he might bump into. Then, in the distance, somebody emerged from the smoke. It was the last person he expected to find here, and he bleeped in shock. Before him stood Optimus Prime!

Bumblebee beeped a hello to Optimus, but received no response. The Autobot leader didn't even didn't seem able to see his old friend.

Ratchet explained, 'Bumblebee, that is not Optimus! It's just a figment of Megatron's mind. It cannot see or hear you.'

Bumblebee looked up at Optimus in disappointment. It had been nice to see a friendly face in this horrible place. But then he heard a distinctly *unfriendly* laugh echo around the plaza and looked up to see Megatron on a ledge high above them.

'Optimus Prime!' called Megatron. 'Your

Autobot armies are defeated. Bow before your new master!'

Bumblebee stood aside. He seemed

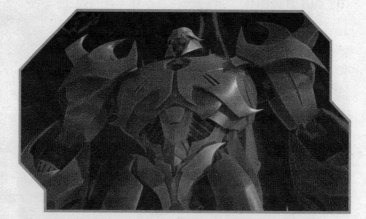

to be viewing some old memory of Megatron's from the Cybertron war. He looked on as Optimus turned bravely to face his old enemy, unsheathing a sword from his arm. 'Never, Megatron! One shall stand and one shall fall!'

'Defiant to the end,' mocked Megatron, unsheathing his own sword. 'So be it.'

With that, he leaped down into the plaza and charged at Optimus. Bumblebee stood aside, ready to see Optimus defend himself, but he watched in horror as Megatron cut down Optimus with one fatal swipe!

The light disappeared from Optimus' eyes and he dropped to the ground.

Back in the Autobot lab, Bulkhead was confused. 'That never happened!' he said.

'It is not a memory,' explained Ratchet. 'We are seeing Kaon as Megatron has recreated it in his darkest dreams.'

Bumblebee ran over to the body of Optimus, but before he could get there, Optimus was back on his feet, somehow alive again. Megatron's mind had brought him back to fight all over again!

'Megatron, your treachery ends here!' yelled Optimus.

Megatron turned round and smiled. He raised his blaster arm and charged it, ready to fire. Projection or not, Bumblebee wasn't about to watch his leader get killed

all over again! He leaped bravely in front
of Optimus just as Megatron fired. But the
laser shot straight past Bumblebee and hit
the fake Optimus, who fell to the ground
once again.

Bumblebee turned in despair to see
Megatron looming over him. He was
looking straight at him!

'The Autobot scout,' said Megatron
in recognition. Optimus might not have
been able to see him, but it seemed that
Megatron could! Bumblebee backed away,
but it was too late.

'The penalty for trespassing in

my domain is *destruction*!' screamed Megatron as he raised his sword high over his head and brought it straight down at Bumblebee!

CHAPTER SIX

GET OUT OF MY HEAD!

Megatron stared down at Bumblebee in
confusion. The Autobot ought to be lying
in two pieces at his feet right now. Instead,
Megatron's blade had passed straight
through him without harm, as if he wasn't
even there.

'How can this be?' wondered Megatron.

Bumblebee checked himself over for
damage, but he seemed to be unharmed.
He bleeped to show that he was just as
confused as Megatron.

Megatron decided to test the matter
further, and launched a wave of attacks
on Bumblebee. All of them passed straight

through the Autobot, as if he were no more than a ghost.

Back at the Autobot HQ, a slightly shaken Raf was trying to understand what was happening. 'So, Megatron can't touch Bee?' he asked.

'No,' explained Ratchet. 'He is *not* a creation of Megatron's mind, so he is immune to his physical attacks.'

After a few more strikes, Megatron gave up attacking Bumblebee and tried to work out what was going on. He looked the Autobot scout up and down, and ticked off the possibilities.

'You are *not* wearing Phase Displacement Armour. Your eyes track my movement, so you are *not* a hologram, and I do not believe in spirits. So tell me, "Scout", *What are you?*'

A loud and booming voice interrupted them. '*Megatron!*'

Megatron and Bumblebee looked across the plaza to see Optimus Prime, alive again and ready to attack, but this time he had brought back-up. Bulkhead and another Bumblebee!

'Uh-oh, special guest stars!' called out Miko. Ratchet shook his head at the monitor. 'This is not good . . .' he realized. If Megatron came to understand that he was in a coma, it might make it harder for Bumblebee to find the information he needed.

Inside Megatron's mind, Bumblebee ran over to the new arrivals. He was glad of the help, but they did not seem to see him. He waved in front of the other Bumblebee's face, but he was only a projection of Megatron's mind, just like before.

Megatron's head was hurting from trying to work this out, so he let his blaster do the thinking for him. He raised his arm and fired a wave of shots at Optimus, Bulkhead and the two Bumblebees. When the smoke finally cleared, all that remained was the avatar of Bumblebee.

Megatron looked at him in amazement. He was starting to work this out. 'You are real . . . but *they* were not!' Megatron laughed a deep and sinister chuckle as he realized what must be going on.

'A Cortical-Psychic patch! How *unexpected*.'

Ratchet looked at his monitor in growing horror. 'We've stirred Megatron from his oblivion. He's becoming self-aware!'

Megatron paced around the plaza and considered what all this must mean. He turned to Bumblebee in anger. 'But if this is my subconscious, *what are you doing inside my head?*'

Back in the Decepticon lab on board the *Nemesis,* Arcee was looking down at Bumblebee's real body with concern. 'Come on, Bee, what are you doing in there? Hurry!'

A noise from behind distracted her as the doors to the lab slid open. Starscream and Knockout came into the room, with Soundwave following closely behind them. Starscream approached Megatron's sickbed to check on the patient. He was ready to put his plan into action and be rid of Megatron, once and for all!

'Knockout, if you would be so kind as to provide your expert medical opinion to Soundwave. For the *historical record*.' Starscream's voice dripped with phoney concern.

Arcee ducked down as low as she could behind Megatron's sick bed, but luckily the Decepticons didn't seem to have noticed her yet. She listened carefully as Knockout started to talk.

'Simply put, unaided by these machines, Megatron could remain in this deathless slumber for ever.'

Starscream shook his head and struggled to keep the smile from his face. 'Our Master would not have wanted to be seen this way!' he said. 'To stand idly by while he remains a captive in his own body is not just!'

Soundwave looked at them both suspiciously. He was not easily fooled, and he knew just how much Starscream wanted to become the permanent leader of the Decepticons. Silently, he pointed at the brainwave monitor that stood by Megatron's bed. The red wavy line was still going up and down rapidly.

'That's just brainwave activity,' said Knockout, dismissively, 'not evidence of "consciousness", but merely of an endless dream from which Megatron may never wake.'

Starscream shook his head sadly. 'Soundwave, we must face reality. Megatron is lost to us.'

'The only honourable option would be to show him mercy,' added Knockout.

'A simple throw of the switch . . .' suggested Starscream.

'It would be quick, painless and compassionate . . .' continued Knockout.

Soundwave considered their words. He didn't trust either of them for a moment. But he did not like to see his Master reduced to this state either. Perhaps there was some truth in what they were saying?

Arcee listened to their conversation in growing horror. If they were about to pull the plug on Megatron, then what would happen to Bumblebee? She whispered into her comm-link, 'Ratchet, are you hearing all this?'

Ratchet nodded. 'If Megatron perishes, then Bumblebee's mind will remain separated from his body for ever!'

'We'll lose Bumblebee as well as Optimus!' exclaimed Jack.

CHAPTER SEVEN

BARGAINING WITH MEGATRON

Inside Megatron's mind, Megatron loomed over Bumblebee. He knew that the only possible explanation for why he couldn't hurt Bumblebee was that Bee had entered his mind. But he also knew that if that were true, then he must be lying unconscious somewhere . . .

'The only way you could have entered my mind is via a Cortical–Psychic patch,' he said. 'But the question remains, *what happened to me?*'

As Megatron stared into Bumblebee's eyes, his memories suddenly started to flood back to him.

*He had been on the Spacebridge, doing
battle with the Autobots. He had gone back
to Cybertron and used Dark Energon to
raise an army of Terrorcons that were ready
to attack the Earth. But then something
had gone wrong, and there had been a huge
explosion . . .*

'A Spacebridge explosion!' said Megatron.
Surely there was no way he could have
survived such an event? 'And yet, if you
are in my head, I am not "one with the
AllSpark". So tell me, Scout, do I still
function?'

Bumblebee looked up at Megatron in
desperation. He didn't know what to
say, and this conversation wasn't getting
him any closer to finding a cure for
Optimus!

Ratchet's voice crackled over the comm-
link, 'Bumblebee, we are out of time!'

Bumblebee thought desperately. He
decided there was nothing else for it
but to tell Megatron exactly why he was

there. He bleeped a hasty explanation.

'You search for a cure to the Cybonic plague?' said Megatron as a smile began to creep across his face. 'So someone else besides myself is unwell?'

When Megatron saw the hurt in Bumblebee's eyes, he knew exactly who must have been infected. 'Optimus!' he said, and then began to laugh loudly when Bumblebee nodded. 'Such irony, that after ages of endless battle, the mighty Optimus Prime is felled by a simple virus from the distant past!' But did this Autobot scout, who had *dared*

to enter his mind, actually imagine that Megatron might be willing to *help* him? 'And what makes you think I would save the life of my oldest enemy?'

Bumblebee thought for a moment, but he couldn't come up with one good reason. Megatron had been trying to destroy Optimus for years, and now all he had to do was sit back and victory would be his. Bumblebee was stumped.

Just then, another image of Optimus Prime appeared across the plaza. It started to speak, but without even looking up, Megatron raised his blaster and shot it

down once again.

Bumblebee stared in disgust and amazement. Why was Megatron so obsessed with destroying Optimus over and over again? With a flash he realized that there was something that Megatron wanted even more than to see Optimus dead. He bleeped at Megatron.

'Oh?' replied Megatron. 'And just what is it that I want the most?'

Bee explained in a series of high-pitched bleeps. What Megatron wanted more than anything was to be able to destroy Optimus by his own hand!

Megatron laughed. 'But do you not see? Inside my mind, I *do* slay Optimus by my own hand! At will, whenever I desire!'

Bumblebee bleeped loudly and insistently. Back in the Autobot base, Raf translated his words for the others.

'Bee told Megatron that if he lets the plague virus destroy the *real* Optimus, then Megatron will never get the chance to do it himself.'

'That's smart!' said Jack.

'That's *twisted*!' added Miko, impressed.

Back in the *Nemesis* laboratory, Soundwave was still staring silently at Megatron. Starscream was growing impatient.

'Soundwave, do I take your silence to mean that you agree with Knockout's medical expertise?'

Soundwave just carried on staring. He didn't like what was happening, but he had to admit that Megatron was in a bad condition. Maybe it would be best to let him go?

Starscream started to reach for the large tube that connected Megatron's spark chamber to his life-support systems. All he had to do was pull out the tube, and that would be the end of Megatron. 'Speak now, or for ever hold your peace,' he warned.

Arcee watched in terror from her hiding

spot. If Starscream pulled out that tube, then Bumblebee would be trapped! She had to do something. She raised her blaster and carefully aimed it at Starscream.

Starscream's hand hovered over the tube. 'Going . . . going . . .' he teased. But Soundwave wasn't looking at Megatron any more. He'd seen something strange on the floor behind the sick bed, and he pointed.

'What is it?' asked Starscream, before turning to see a strange cable leading from Megatron's head; it hadn't been there earlier. Starscream picked it up.

Arcee watched helplessly as the

Decepticons discovered the cable she had plugged into Megatron to activate the Cortical-Psychic patch. All they had to do was follow it, and it would lead them right to her position! '*Scrap!*' she cursed under her breath. She looked over at Bumblebee and hoped he was hurrying up in there . . .

CHAPTER EIGHT

ONE BRAIN TO ANOTHER

Deep inside Megatron's mind, Megatron was coming to a decision about Optimus. He had to admit, the Autobot scout had a point. 'After our deep history together, to not watch the spark ebb from Optimus' eyes with my own ...' He looked down at

Bumblebee, his mind made up. 'Well played, Scout.'

Megatron extended a hand to Bumblebee and a rotating hologram in the shape of a cube appeared in his hand. The cube glowed green, and Bumblebee could see that it was full of data.

'This is the chemical formula for the cure you seek,' explained Megatron. 'Not that I expect you to know how to read it.'

Megatron was right. Bumblebee had no idea what it said! But he knew that Ratchet would be able to interpret it, so he reached out to take it from Megatron.

'Not yet!' said Megatron, pulling the cube away. 'How am I to accomplish terminating Optimus, as you propose, while trapped here inside a perpetual daydream? You will only have the cure once you release me from this prison! You must guarantee my recovery or Optimus fades to gun-metal grey!'

But Ratchet was way ahead of Megatron. Back at the Autobot base, he was rewinding the recording of everything that Bumblebee had seen inside Megatron's head. He paused it over an image of the rotating green cube and zoomed in, extracting the data for the cure!

Once finished, he yelled into his comm-link excitedly, 'Arcee, we have the formula! Disconnect Bumblebee from the Cortical-Psychic patch *now*!'

In the Decepticon lab, Arcee quickly reached over and started to detach the cable from the back of Bumblebee's head. The effect inside Megatron's mind was immediate. The image of the city of Kaon began to fall apart in a swirl of colour that formed a whirlwind around them. The avatar image of Bumblebee started to fade away.

'What?' screamed Megatron in fury. '*You were watching! You tricked me!*'

Bumblebee faded into a cloud of dust, and the whirlwind that was the city of Kaon formed a long tunnel portal behind him, sucking the dust cloud into the void.

'*No!*' screamed Megatron. '*Take me with you! Take me!*'

His body also dissolved into a cloud of dust, and it shot off into the portal after Bumblebee, as Kaon fell into chaos.

Onboard the *Nemesis*, the Decepticons were edging closer and closer to Arcee's hiding place. Arcee took the last cable out of Bumblebee and shook him, trying to wake him up. 'Hurry, Bee . . .'

Suddenly Starscream poked his head

down under Megatron's bed and looked Arcee directly in the eye. 'What in . . . *Intruders!*' he yelled as the lights in Bumblebee's eyes came on and he jolted awake.

Without losing a moment, Ratchet reactivated the GroundBridge portal right behind them, and Bumblebee jumped straight through, back to the Autobot base.

Arcee, however, wasn't about to pass up a chance to defeat their most terrible enemy, once and for all. She aimed her blaster carefully at the tube connecting

Megatron's spark chamber to his life-support systems. 'Allow me!' she said, and then fired.

Arcee's shot was on target, and it knocked the tube out of Megatron's spark chamber just as she leaped into the portal, which snapped shut behind her.

As Megatron's life-support machine gave a long, unbroken bleep, Starscream could hardly keep the smile from his face. It looked as if those Autobots had actually been useful for once. He put on a sympathetic tone. 'It was the inevitable outcome,' he said.

But Soundwave wasn't going to let Megatron go that easily! He pointed urgently at the disconnected tube.

Starscream sighed, 'Of course, it would be *wrong* to allow Megatron to perish by an Autobot's hands.'

He gestured to Knockout, who set to work reconnecting Megatron's life-support machine. The monitors leaped back into

life and Megatron's life signs seemed
to stabilize, but the brainwave monitor
remained silent.

'How is the patient doing?' asked
Starscream.

Knockout examined the monitors closely.
'Not sure what the Bots did in there, but
Megatron is registering zero brainwave
activity.'

Starscream considered this. 'Meaning?' he
asked.

'Meaning that physically he's stable, but
now there's "no one home".'

Starscream pondered this. If Megatron

wasn't in his body any more, then where was he?

In the sick bay of Autobot Outpost Omega One, Ratchet put an arm under Optimus and helped him to his feet. 'That's it – steady!'

The cure seemed to have taken effect almost instantly, and already Optimus was starting to look like his old self again.

Ratchet helped him out of the sick bay, where the Autobots and the kids all cheered to see their leader alive and well.

'Please, save the hero's welcome for my

physician and my scout!' said Optimus, gesturing towards Ratchet and Bumblebee. Bumblebee bleeped excitedly and took a bow as his friends cheered loudly.

In their excitement, none of Bumblebee's friends noticed when his face suddenly went blank. The Autobots carried on celebrating while Bumblebee stared off into the distance. It was as if he was feeling nothing at all.

Something was *horribly* wrong. Deep inside Bumblebee's head, in a place behind his darkest dreams, a laugh that was not Bee's own sounded from out of the darkness. It was Megatron! He had used the Cortical-Psychic patch to hitch a ride out of his body and into Bumblebee's head.

'I'm out!' Megatron laughed. 'Or should I say, *in*?'

Check out these other books, for some more action-packed stories!

MEGATRON
RETURNS

OPTIMUS
UNDER THREAT

BULKHEAD'S
BIGGEST BATTLE

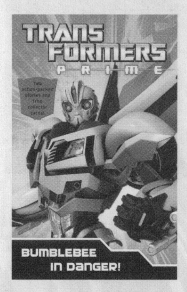

BUMBLEBEE
IN DANGER!

Don't miss any of the action with these awesome new Transformers Prime titles!